PJMASKS
5-MINUTE STORIES

SIMON SPOTLIGHT

New York London Toronto Sydney New Delhi

SIMON SPOTLIGHT

An imprint of Simon & Schuster Children's Publishing Division
1230 Avenue of the Americas, New York, New York 10020

This Simon Spotlight edition December 2018

Contents

Meet the Heroes . . . and the Villains, Too!

Meet the Heroes!

Night in the city, and a brave band of heroes is ready to face fiendish villains to stop them messing with your day . . .

Connor becomes Catboy!

"I'm the cat's whiskers!"

When this cat is let out of the bag, there's no stopping him. Calling on his **Super Cat Speed** and **Super Cat Jump**, Catboy is quick in every way: on his feet, leaping through the air, or zipping around the city behind the wheel of the **Cat-Car**. And with his incredible **Cat Ears** that can hear an evil laugh from miles away, the baddies can't keep any secrets from him!

Amaya becomes Owlette!

Flying through the air with her **Super Owl Wings** or piloting the **Owl Glider**, Owlette will swoop, swirl, and flip her way through any obstacles to help her team. The baddies can run, but they can't hide from Owlette's amazing **Owl Eyes** that can see trouble happening all over the city. And if the baddies do get in her way, Owlette flaps her wings and sends them flying with her **Owl Wing Wind!**

"Fluttering feathers!"

Greg becomes Gekko!

"Cool chameleons!"

Now you see him, now you don't. That's because Gekko has **Super Gekko Camouflage** and can change color to blend in anywhere. Gekko might be the smallest of these three heroes, but with his **Super Gekko Muscles**, he's also the strongest. Whether he's in the **Gekko-Mobile** or using his **Super Lizard Grip** to scale even the highest buildings, Gekko is super awesome.

But just who are
these villains?

PJ Masks, we're on
our way! Into the
night to save
the day!

Romeo

"You may have won this time, but I'll be back!"

Romeo can be found driving around the city in his portable **lab**, inventing machines and all sorts of gadgets to do his bidding. But this mad scientist wants one thing and one thing only . . . **to rule the world!** Fortunately for the world, Romeo is no match for the PJ Masks. He's never won against them yet, but don't expect him to stop trying!

"I'll get you next time, PJ Pests!"

Luna Girl

Luna Girl wants it all—even if that includes things that aren't hers! Using her ultrapowerful **Luna Magnet**, Luna Girl can steal anything for herself. Along with her **moths**, she flies everywhere on her **Luna Board**, causing mischief. That's where the PJ Masks come in: They are always ready to put things right after Luna Girl has done wrong!

If there's one thing Night Ninja is best at, it's thinking he is the best at everything! With his **Ninjalinos** and an unlimited supply of **Sticky-Splats**, Night Ninja is a formidable foe. But then again, Night Ninja's overconfidence always gets in his way, making it easier for the PJ Masks to make a mess of his plans.

"My plan is brilliant! Mwa-ha-ha-ha!"

Night Ninja

PJ Masks all shout hooray!
'Cause in the night,
we saved the day!

Meet Catboy!

Hi, I'm Connor. By day, I'm a kid just like you! I love to have fun with my two best friends, Greg and Amaya.

But by night, I become Catboy—a hero who defends fun for everyone!

While the city sleeps, I face off against Romeo, Night Ninja, and Luna Girl. They hatch plans at night to ruin everyone's day! **It's a catastrophe!**

I have a super team to help me—my best friends! Greg becomes Gekko. Amaya becomes Owlette. Together, we are the PJ Masks. **PJ Masks, we're on our way! Into the night to save the day!**

As Catboy, I have amazing superpowers. I can hear trouble anywhere in the city using my **Cat Ears**!

And you can count on me to be first on the scene with my **Super Cat Speed!**

Plus I can jump really high using my **Super Cat Leap!**

With my catlike reflexes, I can dodge anything the villains throw at me. **Catboy swings in to save the day!**

When the whole team needs to move fast, I press a special button on the PJ Picture Player and call out, "**To the Cat-Car!**"

The only thing that can stop me is . . . water. Ugh, **fur-balls**! I hate getting wet, but not as much as I hate letting my friends down!

We may be super, but our true power is friendship. When the PJ Masks work together, we are unstoppable!
PJ Masks go!

PJ Masks all shout hooray!
'Cause in the night,
we saved the day!

Meet Owlette!

Hi there! I'm Owlette, and I'm on a mission. Would you like to come along? Hold on to your pj's! **Because nighttime is the right time to fight crime!**

I'm a regular kid, just like you! My real name is Amaya, and these are my best friends, Greg and Connor. But when someone messes with our day, we become . . .

. . . Gekko, Owlette, and Catboy! **PJ Masks, we're on our way! Into the night to save the day!**

Fluttering feathers! Luna Girl is messing with the weather. She'll ruin the fun for everyone! We must stop her.

"**To the Owl Glider!**" I say. We go to the top of Headquarters, hop in, buckle up, and take off!

I hope you're not afraid of heights! In the **Owl Glider**, we soar, swoop, and zip to the scene.

Now it's time to use my superpowers! Bad guys can't hide from my **Owl Eyes**!

And when you need superspeed, I'm your hero! I can fly with the fastest plane with my **Super Owl Wings!**

Plus, trouble doesn't stand a chance against my **Owl Wing Wind**! Baddies, be gone!

Whoops! Sometimes I forget to look before I leap. It's a good thing my true power is . . .

. . . teamwork! With my friends by my side, slipups are easy to fix up. Better luck next time, Luna!

Now take a deep breath and help us say "PJ Masks all shout hooray! 'Cause in the night, we saved the day!"

Meet Gekko!

Leaping lizards! I almost didn't see you there! Hi, I'm Greg, and these are my friends Amaya and Connor.

I also have a pet gecko named Lionel. Lionel and I have a lot in common. That's because . . .

. . . at night, I become the supercool hero Gekko! Amaya becomes Owlette, and Connor becomes Catboy! Together, we are the PJ Masks! We go into the night to save the day!

When we need a vehicle that can get us out of sticky situations, I call out, **"To the Gekko-Mobile!"**

The Gekko-Mobile is a lot like me: It is a master of camouflage, can climb the side of a building, and can even glide underwater.

Slithering serpents! I forgot to tell you that as Gekko, I have amazing superpowers.

Nighttime is the right time to fight crime, and that's when I use my **Super Lizard Grip** to climb up walls and stick to ceilings.

I can also walk on ice without slipping.
Cool chameleons, right?

I might be the smallest and the youngest of my friends, but that doesn't stop me from saving the day! That's because I am really strong. I have **Super Gekko Muscles!**

Need to blend in? I'm your hero! I use my **Super Gekko Camouflage** when I need to escape a baddie! But the truth is, I wouldn't be half the hero I am without . . .

. . . my friends! When Owlette, Catboy, and I work together, baddies like Luna Girl, Romeo, and Night Ninja don't stand a chance!

PJ Masks all shout hooray! 'Cause in the night, we saved the day! All it takes is teamwork!

Super Team

It's Sports Day in the park, and Greg, Connor, and Amaya are on their way. But before they arrive, they discover that Sports Day has been canceled. All the gear has disappeared!

"How am I going to get strong in the daytime?" asks Greg.

"Don't worry," says Amaya, "you'll be strong tonight."

"And then we'll find out where the sports equipment has gone," adds Connor.

"PJ Masks, we're on our way!
Into the night to save the day!"
Amaya becomes Owlette!
Greg becomes Gekko!
Connor becomes Catboy!

"Whoever took the sports gear made a big mistake," says Gekko at headquarters. "They're going to find out just how super strong I am! To the Gekko-Mobile!"

Gekko jumps behind the wheel of the Gekko-Mobile and zooms out of headquarters.

"Slithering serpents!" he shouts. "Just let me get at that villain."

Catboy hears something with his Super Cat Ears. "That way!" he tells Gekko.

The PJ Masks hear singing. *La-la, la-la, la-la-la!*
"I recognize those voices!" says Owlette.

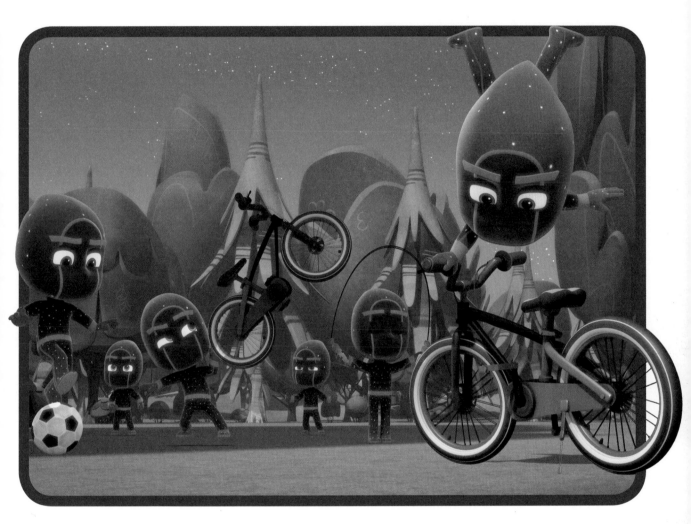

It's Night Ninja and his Ninjalinos! They have all the sports gear. The Ninjalinos are using it to become stronger and stronger. Now they are Super-Ninjalinos! They're almost as strong as Night Ninja.

"They'll never be as strong as me," says Gekko. Just as Owlette and Catboy are about to swoop in and grab the gear back, Gekko stops them. He wants to face the Super-Ninjalinos all by himself.

"Give that sports stuff back, Night Ninja!" says Gekko.

But the Super-Ninjalinos are stronger than he thought. Gekko goes flying.

Gekko has another idea. He'll build a trap. The Super-Ninjalinos will walk right into it.

"Are you sure we can't help, Gekko?" asks Owlette.

"I'm fine," Gekko replies. "This plan is all about my super strength! You guys just stand back. Super Gekko Muscles!"

He pulls a rope and traps the Super-Ninjalinos in a box. The box hangs from a high tree branch.

But Night Ninja isn't concerned. "You PJ Masks are exhausting. Jump, Super-Ninjalinos," he commands.

Inside the box, the Super-Ninjalinos all jump at the same time. Gekko is still holding on to the rope. As the Super-Ninjalinos come down in the box, Gekko is hurled up onto the tree branch!

"It really does seem like we ninjas do this 'strong' thing better than you," taunts Night Ninja.

"Don't worry. We've got this," Catboy assures Gekko.

"No, I've got this," says Gekko, jumping down from the tree. "Want someone strong to practice with, Night Ninja? Well, here I come!"

"Super-Ninjalinos, get him!" Night Ninja orders. The Super-Ninjalinos rush toward Gekko and carry him off. "Put me down!" cries Gekko. But instead, the Super-Ninjalinos toss Gekko high into the air.

"Are you all right?" asks Catboy as he and Owlette catch Gekko.

"No," Gekko replies. "I should have just let you help me. The Super-Ninjalinos are so strong that no one can stop them."

"Especially when they're all together," adds Catboy.

"That's it!" shouts Gekko. "The Ninjalinos are stronger when they're together, but so are we! It's time to be a hero!"

The PJ Masks gather all the Sports Day equipment they can find.

"Hey, Ninjalinos," Gekko calls to them. "There's still some sports gear that you don't have."

The Super-Ninjalinos rush toward the heroes!

The PJ Masks split up. So do the Super-Ninjalinos. Now Gekko, Owlette, and Catboy are each facing just a few of them. They are no match for the PJ Masks! One by one, Gekko tosses them back into the trap he'd made before. Now the heroes can take the sports equipment back where it belongs.

"PJ Masks all shout hooray! 'Cause in the night, we saved the day!"

Sports Day is saved, all thanks to the PJ Masks!

"Now everyone is going to get fit and strong after all!" says Greg. He lifts a bike . . . with the help of his friends.

"You don't need to be *that* strong," Connor reminds him.

"Not when you've got friends to help you!" adds Amaya.

PJ Masks Make Friends!

Connor, Greg, and Amaya are visiting the zoo.
"Greg and I want to see the butterflies," Amaya says.
"Butterflies?" Connor says. "No way! They just flap around.
I want to see the big cats—with their big teeth and claws!" He
jumps up and roars.

"Connor! Stop being so rough," Amaya says. "*We* want to see the butterflies. We can all go and see the lions and tigers later."

Disappointed, Connor follows Greg and Amaya to the butterfly house. But the butterfly house is empty!

"The butterflies are *gone*!" Amaya cries.

Just then, something flutters by. It's a moth!

"Luna Girl!" the three friends say together.

"She must have taken the butterflies," Amaya says.

"PJ Masks, we're on our way!
Into the night to save the day!"
Greg becomes Gekko!
Amaya becomes Owlette!
Connor becomes Catboy!

The PJ Masks begin searching for the missing butterflies right away.

"Over there!" Owlette shouts, using her Owl Eyes.

"A butterfly! It must have escaped from Luna Girl," Gekko says.

Gekko and Owlette try to convince the butterfly to come with them.

Owlette asks the butterfly if it wants to fly with her. Gekko changes his colors to match the butterfly's wings.

"This is taking too long," Catboy complains. "What we need is some . . . *Super Cat Speed*!"

In a flash, Catboy grabs a small net and a box with some holes in it. He zips around Gekko and Owlette and shoves the lonely butterfly into the box.

"You were really rough, Catboy," Owlette says. "You're making it unhappy."

"But this is the best way to get it home," Catboy says. "And there are more to catch. Look! *Super Cat Speed!*"

Catboy zooms toward the butterflies with his net!

The box shimmies and shakes on the ground. "Catboy! Can't you be gentle? You're making those butterflies really miserable!" Owlette says.

"But I'm *helping* them," Catboy says. "Now, where's Luna Girl with the others?"

Suddenly, the PJ Masks see a cloud of moths in the sky.

"Fly away!" a voice near them shouts. "I don't need you anymore."

It's Luna Girl!

"You've messed up enough, measly moths—time to try some new *butterfly* sidekicks," she says.

"Not so fast, Luna Girl! The PJ Masks are here to take those butterflies back!" says Catboy.

Luna Girl looks at her moths.

"Oh, all right, moths. *One* last chance—get rid of these PJ pests!" she tells them.

The moths swarm around Owlette and Gekko.

Luna Girl sets her eyes on Catboy.

"Get him, Butterfly Brigade," she tells the butterflies, "or you'll be trapped by my Luna-Magnet forever!"

The butterflies zoom toward Catboy.

"Catboy to the rescue!" Catboy shouts.

Quickly, he uses his net to capture the butterflies. But they don't like being caught. Some of them escape!

"Whoa! Where do you think you're going?" Catboy asks. He accidentally knocks over the box with the rest of the butterflies . . . and now they *all* escape!

Catboy tries recapturing the butterflies with his net.
"Stop being so rough!" Owlette calls out.
But it's too late—the butterflies are mad. They push
Catboy, and he falls down, hard.

"Take *that*, Catboy!" Luna Girl shouts triumphantly. She turns to the moths. "See, you useless moths, *that's* how it's done!"

Catboy is confused. "But I was trying to save the butterflies," he says.

"Maybe they're angry at being put in a box," Gekko suggests.

"No one likes being shoved around," Owlette says. "Did *you*?"

Catboy realizes that Gekko and Owlette are right. "I *was* rough with them," he admits. "But when they were rough with me, I didn't like it at all!"

Luna Girl points a finger at the PJ Masks.
"Go on, Butterfly Brigade! Get them!"
But the butterflies swarm her instead.
"They don't like Luna Girl being rough with them either!"
Catboy realizes. "It's time to be a hero!"

Catboy leaps up and uses his *Super Cat Speed*! With a flash of blue light, he gathers a bunch of flowers for the butterflies to eat.

"I'm really sorry about before, butterflies," Catboy says. "I've brought you as many flowers as I could find. *Please* come with us...."

One butterfly lands on a flower. Then the rest follow!

"Wait! Butterflies—you can't go with them!" Luna Girl calls out. But the butterflies continue to follow the PJ Masks—and her moths do too!

"No! No! No! Now I haven't got *any* helpers." Luna Girl sniffles. "I'm sorry, moths."

Luna Girl was rough to her moths, so they left her. But now that she is being gentle, her moths return to her side.

Catboy realizes that being nice and gentle is how you make friends.

And today, the PJ Masks made lots of friends!

PJ Masks all shout hooray!
'Cause in the night,
we saved the day!

Into the Night to Save the Day!

Connor, Greg, and Amaya are playing outside with their flying discs. "Kicking Cartwheel!" Amaya cheers as she catches the disc.

"Swirling Spin!" Greg shouts, catching another. Greg throws his disc to Connor, but it soars into the garden instead. Connor runs after it.

When Connor returns, his friends are gone! Their two flying discs are on the ground, and there's a circuit board underneath them. What could a circuit board be doing there?

"This is a mission for the PJ Masks!" Connor says. "Well, one of us, anyway. This PJ Mask is on his way . . . into the night to save the day!"

Connor becomes Catboy!

Catboy analyzes the circuit board with the PJ Picture Player. The circuit board is from a robot, and a robot means Romeo is behind this!

Catboy speeds through the city in his Cat-Car to track down Romeo.

"Romeo!" Catboy shouts when he finds the troublemaker. "What have you done with my friends?"

"They're here," Romeo sneers, "but they work for me now!"

"We will only obey Romeo," Owlette says.

Just then Catboy hears a noise overhead.

Catboy looks up—Greg and Amaya are trapped in cages! Amaya explains that Romeo captured them when they were playing outside.

"But if you're in those cages, who are they?" asks Catboy, pointing toward Gekko and Owlette.

That's when Catboy realizes—they aren't Gekko and Owlette. They're robots!

"If I hadn't lost my circuit board, you would have been a robot too!" Romeo says.

"You mean this?" says Catboy. He holds up the circuit board he found.

Romeo's eyes widen. "Soon my Robo-Owl and Robo-Gekko will put you in a cage too!"

"Catboy, free us so we can help you!" Amaya calls from her cage.

"Not without your powers!" Catboy shouts back. "But don't worry. I'll get your pajamas back from Romeo!"

Catboy leaps into the Cat-Car to get away from the robots, but he lands upside down. Robo-Gekko jumps into the passenger seat beside him and pushes the eject button.

Catboy's seat flies out of the car, and the robots drive the Cat-Car back to Romeo!

"Look!" Greg shouts as he watches the robots pull up. "They took Catboy's Cat-Car!"

"I know we can help Catboy, even without our powers . . . ," Amaya says sadly.

Greg has an idea! "Let's take this cage apart. Give me your hairpin so I can unscrew this bar."

Catboy arrives on the scene. "Stop trying to escape," he whispers to his friends. "Without your powers you'll be safer up here."

But then Catboy loses his balance and falls. Romeo sees what they're up to and sends in his robots!

"At least I still have this," Catboy says, pulling out the circuit board. But Robo-Gekko swipes it right out of his hand!

"Now that I have the missing piece, I can activate my Robo-Cat! Mwa-ha-ha-ha!" Romeo laughs.

He slides open the door in his lab and reveals—Robo-Cat!

Catboy needs to take back Greg's and Amaya's pajamas so they can become Gekko and Owlette, but Romeo has other ideas.

"Robo-Cat, lock that pussycat up," Romeo commands.

Just then a flying disc appears! It knocks Robo-Cat off his feet.

"Greg and Amaya to the rescue!" Amaya shouts.

Catboy looks behind him and sees . . . Greg and Amaya, standing free!

Catboy smiles. "You guys really are amazing—even without your powers. You were right. I *should* have let you help out."

Before Greg and Amaya can respond, Romeo commands Robo-Gekko and Robo-Owl to catch the heroes.

"It's time to be a hero and let you guys help," Catboy tells his friends. "Super Cat Speed!" He zips past the robots, grabs the pajamas, and gives them to his friends.

Gleefully, Greg and Amaya put their pajamas on.

Greg becomes Gekko!
Amaya becomes Owlette!

"We need to get to Romeo's supercomputer to stop the robots," Owlette says.

But then the robots tackle her and Gekko. Catboy can't tell his friends apart from the robots!

"Now what, kitty-litter boy?" Romeo says, delighted.

"Your robots may have superpowers, but they're not *friends* like we are!" Catboy says. He flings two metal lids into the air, just like flying discs!

"Kicking Cartwheel!" the real Owlette shouts.

"Swirling Spin!" the real Gekko cheers.

"See, Romeo? I know who my friends are. Ready for our special move?" Catboy says.

He flings his metal lid at the rope that holds up Amaya's and Greg's cages. The cages fall and trap Robo-Gekko!

Owlette and Gekko throw their lids and knock out Robo-Owl and Robo-Cat!

Then Catboy throws another lid directly at Romeo's supercomputer. . . .

BAM! The robots power down, this time for good.

"No! My supercomputer!" Romeo cries. "You'll pay for this next time, PJ Masks!"

The PJ Masks watch as Romeo takes off in his lab.

"Looks like Romeo won't be back for a while, now that his supercomputer has been destroyed," Catboy says happily. "With or without our superpowers, we're an amazing team."

**PJ Masks all shout hooray!
'Cause in the night,
we saved the day!**

PJ Masks and the Dinosaur!

Connor, Greg, and Amaya are visiting the museum. "Come on!" Greg says. "The museum's got a new dinosaur show with a big flying pterodactyl!"

"Wow!" Connor and Amaya say. The three friends rush inside.

"Amaya!" Greg calls. "Hurry up!"

"Where's Connor?" Amaya asks. Just then she sees a Tyrannosaurus rex lurching toward her.

"Rrroooar!" says the dinosaur.

"Aaaaarrrgh!" Amaya screams as she stumbles backward into a model Tyrannosaurus rex skeleton.

The model Tyrannosaurus rex skull falls on Amaya. Connor steps out from behind the cardboard dinosaur.

"Oops," he says, trying not to giggle.

"Connor! That wasn't funny!" Amaya says.

"It was a little bit funny," Connor argues.

"Guys!" Greg shouts. "Come quick!"

"What's going on?" Amaya asks.

"The pterodactyl was right there," Greg says. "But someone's taken it!"

"Don't worry," Connor says. "We'll get it back. PJ Masks, we're on our way!"

"Into the night to save the day!" they all say together.

Greg becomes Gekko!
Amaya becomes Owlette!
Connor becomes Catboy!

Under the cover of night, the heroes go in search of the missing pterodactyl. "Okay, Owlette, use your Owl Eyes," Catboy says.

"I will," Owlette says, "once you say you're sorry."

"Oh, you mean for scaring you in the museum?" Catboy asks. "All right, I'm sorry. Now let's go."

"Is that it?" Owlette asks. "That wasn't a very big sorry."

"Guys!" Gekko says, noticing something in the sky.

A robotic pterodactyl swoops down over them with a terrible *screech*!

"Mwa-ha-ha!" Romeo laughs. "Did I make you jump with my robot pterodactyl? I'm the best! Who else could steal a giant model dinosaur and make it fly?"

"But you shouldn't have, Romeo," Gekko says.

"We'll stop you!" Catboy calls.

Just then a cat jumps out of the bushes and surprises Romeo. He loses control of his robot.

"Quick, before Romeo fixes the pterodactyl!" Catboy says. "Let's take him by surprise."

"But first say sorry for surprising me in the museum," Owlette says.

"I said I was sorry," Catboy says with a sigh.

"Fine, I'll just go catch Romeo on my own!" Owlette says, and flies away.

Romeo gets control of his robot. With no time to waste, Catboy and Owlette spring into action at the same time. The two heroes crash in midair. "Oof!" they say, landing on the ground.

"You let Romeo escape!" Owlette says.

Owlette dives at Romeo.

"Whoa!" he says, dropping the remote control.

Gekko catches the remote control. "How about a dino-ride, Gekko style!"

"Let me down!" Romeo yells from the bucking robot.

"Coming in for a landing," Gekko says, making the robot roll. Romeo tumbles onto his lab.

Catboy hangs on as Gekko safely lands the robot. "Nice work, PJ Masks!" Catboy says, but not everyone is happy.

"Just because we beat Romeo," Owlette says, "it doesn't make it all right that you scared me." She flies away more upset than ever.

"Wait, Owlette! Please!" Catboy says. He grabs the remote control from Gekko.

"Catboy!" Gekko calls. "Flying that thing isn't easy!"

"I don't care. I have to catch up with Owlette and make up!" Catboy says. "By my cat's whiskers . . . whoa!" The robot flips upside down, and Catboy drops the remote control.

The remote control falls right into Romeo's hands!
"Now I'll get my pterodactyl back and catch Catboy,
too!" he sneers. "Mwa-ha-ha!"

From a distant rooftop Owlette hears Catboy's yells.

"Help!" he calls to Owlette. "I took the pterodactyl to catch up with you to make sure we were still friends! But now Romeo's in control again!"

"Of course we are still friends!" she says. "This is all my fault. I should have made up with you before. Time to be a hero!"

"That's it, Romeo!" Owlette yells. "No one messes with my friend!" She flies to Catboy's rescue. "Grab on to me!" she says to Catboy.

Catboy hangs on to Owlette as she lifts him off the pterodactyl. "Get him!" she says, and Catboy gives the pterodactyl a mighty kick.

"Aaagh!" Romeo yells as the pterodactyl flies right at him. He dives off the roof of his lab and lands in a pile of garbage.

"I think you dropped something, Romeo!" Gekko calls as he grabs the remote control from the ground.

"What?" Romeo says. Gekko makes the robot chase him. "No, no, no! Get away!" Romeo whines as he runs off into the distance.

"That's the last we'll see of Romeo for a while!" Owlette says. "Good job, team!"

"Thanks, Owlette," Catboy says.

The heroes learned an important lesson that night. Making up can be tough, but it's what friends do!

PJ Masks all shout hooray!
'Cause in the night,
we saved the day!

Super Moon Adventure

Connor, Greg, and Amaya are on a field trip at the museum. They are visiting the planetary exhibit!

Their teacher points to a big orange sphere above. "This is what a harvest moon looks like. It only happens once a year. And tonight everyone can look out their window and see a real harvest moon for themselves!" he says.

As the class takes a closer look, the three friends hang back. "You know who loves the moon?" asks Connor.

Greg guesses werewolves. But Connor reminds him that Luna Girl would never miss the harvest moon. It is up to them to stop any mischief she might cause.

That night the PJ Masks know what to do. They must protect the harvest moon!

PJ Masks are on their way . . . into the night to save the day!

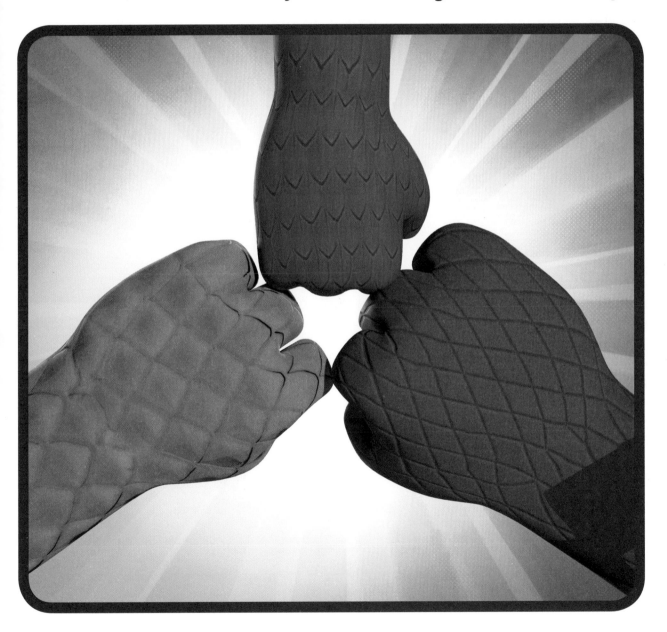

At Headquarters, PJ Robot is ready to help. He
tracks down Luna Girl in the town square. The three
heroes hop into the Cat-Car to catch Luna Girl!

When the PJ Masks arrive at the square, they are mesmerized by what they see above. "Whoa! So that's the harvest moon!" says Gekko.

"Correction. That's *my* harvest moon! Check out how it super-charged my Luna Magnet!" brags Luna Girl.

Now she can fly to the moon and take control of the harvest moon crystal. She points her magnet at the moon and flies toward it.

Back at Headquarters the PJ Masks prepare to follow her—straight into space! It's time to put on their space suits, strap on their seat belts, and count down to liftoff!

"Okay, PJ Robot, begin transformation," says Catboy, and PJ Masks Headquarters changes into . . . the PJ Rocket!

"Let's see what this baby can do," says Owlette. "Who knows what's out there?"

"That's kinda the problem," whispers Gekko as he nervously plots their course.

Luna Girl spots the PJ Rocket! She sends energy bubbles its way. Owlette rolls the ship back and forth. She dodges all the energy bubbles—except one. There's a little damage to the ship. Gekko grows more worried.

"This is gonna get a little bumpy," says Owlette. She sets the ship down onto the moon so PJ Robot can fix it.

Luna Girl lands nearby, and her Luna Magnet pulls her across the moon's surface. The PJ Masks watch on the PJ Player. They get ready to follow her. But Gekko is worried.

"I've never been away from home before. I'm scared we're going to be stuck here," he admits.

The team has a new plan. Gekko will guard the ship while Catboy and Owlette jump onto their PJ Rovers and track down Luna Girl.

Using her Owl Eyes, Owlette spots Luna Girl in a crater. "There she is. We better hurry!" she cries.

They arrive just as Luna Girl's magnet fuses with a huge moonstone and transforms into a powerful Luna Wand! Catboy's Super Cat Speed doesn't work as well on the moon. He can't catch Luna Girl! And Owlette's Owl Wing Wind is acting funny too. Yet Luna Girl's powers have grown stronger.

"Sorry, PJ Pests . . . your powers don't work quite the same on the moon," says Luna Girl as she quickly builds a fortress and traps Catboy and Owlette in crystal pods!

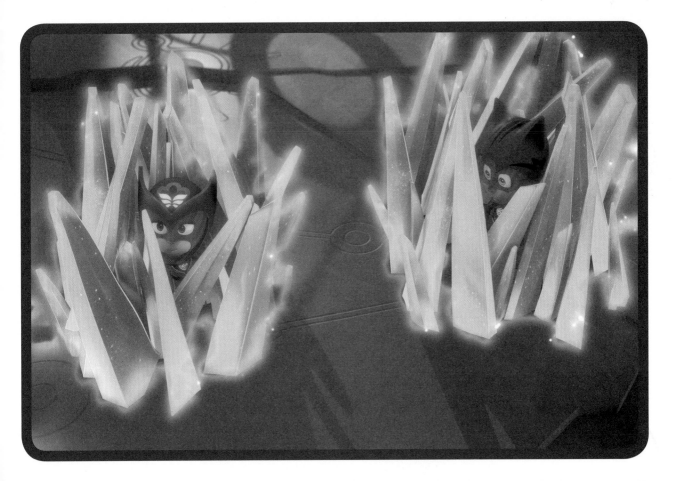

Gekko sees the whole thing on the com-links from his friends' helmets. But then he loses contact! He knows he has to help them, even if it means going out into a place that scares him.

"You can do this!" PJ Robot chirps.

"Time to be a hero," Gekko says as he heads into the dark on his PJ Rover.

Meanwhile, Luna Girl continues to create new things with her Luna Wand, like a throne and a statue of herself.

"I need some royal subjects," Luna Girl says. Then she teases Owlette and Catboy. "Imagine everyone you know and love forced to be my loyal subjects here on the moon—forever!"

Little does she know Gekko is close by! He climbs up the fortress walls.

"Catboy, Owlette . . . can you hear me? Psst! Up here," Gekko whispers to his friends below. Using his Super Gekko Camouflage, he goes into chameleon mode, but he accidentally sets off an alarm. With a wave of her wand, Luna Girl reveals Gekko and traps him in another crystal pod!

After Luna Girl flies away, Catboy uses his Super Cat Speed to create vibrations that can crack the crystal pods!

"Super Gekko Muscles!" grunts Gekko as he tips over his pod onto his friends' pods.

"It's working. It's working!" shouts Owlette.

The vibrations crack open the crystal pods. The PJ Masks are free! But they've also set off an alarm!

PJ Robot transmits good news to the heroes through their com-links. "The ship is fixed!" he chirps.

Just as they're about to head back to the ship, Luna Girl surprises them. Her Luna Wand sends energy blasts straight at the PJ Masks.

This time they're ready. They remove their gravity boots. Their weightlessness on the moon lets Owlette fly through the air while Catboy races all around the fortress. Luna Girl sends another blast right at Gekko!

"Whoa. Don't worry, guys. I've got this," he says.

Gekko uses his Super Gekko Shield to bounce the blast back at Luna Girl, and as she drops her Luna Wand, Owlette swoops in and catches it!

Luna Girl tries to summon the Luna Wand, but the wand has a mind of its own! It starts blasting energy bolts all over the fortress, destroying everything inside.

"No! Stop. You're ruining my precious fortress!" cries Luna Girl.

The harvest moon crystal falls away from the wand.

"I'll take that!" says Owlette as she catches the crystal.

The PJ Masks race back to their ship on their PJ Rovers, bringing the harvest moon crystal with them.

"All fixed and ready to go!" chirps PJ Robot.

It's time to head home!

They aren't the only ones going home. Luna Girl wants to chase after the PJ Masks, but she's lost control of her magnet. It creates an energy bubble that surrounds Luna Girl and slowly takes her back to Earth.

"Aw, come on . . . they're getting away. Faster, you silly Luna Magnet!" she cries.

Back on Earth, the PJ Rocket lands, safe and sound.

"Oh boy! Home, sweet home!" says Gekko as he kisses the ground. "Blech!"

The heroes laugh as PJ Robot places the harvest moon crystal in the vault.

Catboy and Owlette check on their friend. "Are you okay?" asks Owlette.

"It was scary at first, but nothing would be as scary as not being a hero with you guys," Gekko answers.

PJ Masks all shout hooray!
'Cause in the night,
we saved the day!

Owlette Gets a Pet

Amaya and Connor are playing at Greg's house when Greg shows them his pet lizard, Lionel.

"I wish I had a pet," says Amaya. "They're lots of fun."

"Yeah, but they're hard work, too," says Greg.

Amaya smiles. "I guess, but they're *mostly* fun!"

All of a sudden, the friends' bracelets start to flash and buzz.

"It's the alarm signal. Someone's trying to break into HQ!" says Greg.

"PJ Masks, we're on our way! Into the night to save the day!" they all say.

Amaya becomes Owlette!

Connor becomes Catboy!

Greg becomes Gekko!

The intruder isn't a baddie. It's a bird, and Owlette decides it will be her new pet, Birdy! Gekko reminds her that pets are a lot of work, but Owlette isn't worried.

The PJ Masks have no idea that Luna Girl is spying on them with her magical Luna Magnet and wants to teach Owlette a lesson.

Then Gekko notices something on the PJ Picture Player: Luna Girl is taking a vase from the museum, and she is getting away!

"You stay with Birdy," Catboy tells Owlette. "Gekko and I will deal with Luna Girl."

"But I want to come on the mission," says Owlette. "I'm sure Birdy will be fine."

The heroes zoom out of HQ in Owlette's Owl Glider, catch up to Luna Girl, and return the vase to the museum. The PJ Masks have no idea that, back at HQ, Birdy is following orders from Luna Girl, who trained her to place a Luna Crystal in the room. A Luna Beam is shooting out!

When the PJ Masks return, HQ is a mess!

"Birdy, why did you do this?" cries Owlette.

"Maybe because you left her alone," suggests Gekko. "Lionel always makes a mess when I don't pay enough attention to him. Pets are fun, but they need exercise and training and lots of . . ."

Gekko is interrupted by the PJ Picture Player's alarm.

"Luna Girl is at the zoo," says Owlette, and they run toward the exit.

"What about Birdy?" Gekko asks Owlette.

Owlette has an idea. "She can come too. I'll train her as we go!"

Gekko does not think that is a good idea at all!

The heroes find that Luna Girl let the butterflies out of their enclosure! The PJ Masks have to get the butterflies back inside, but Birdy keeps scaring them away, so Owlette puts her in the Owl Glider.

"Birdy only wants some attention," Gekko tells Owlette.

Meanwhile, Luna Girl places two Luna Crystals in Birdy's wings to bring back to HQ so Luna Girl can take control of it.

Once the PJ Masks are finished saving the butterflies, they head back to HQ and notice that Birdy is hungry.

Owlette takes Birdy up to her room to give her some food, but then Luna Girl appears on the Owl Eye screen. Owlette decides to wait to feed Birdy. Right now she has to stop Luna Girl!

While the PJ Masks are gone from HQ, Birdy plants the two Luna Crystals, and purple Luna Beams shoot out of HQ's Owl Eyes. Soon all kinds of things start flying toward HQ!

"I've turned HQ into a giant Luna Magnet," Luna Girl explains. "Thanks to that bird, it'll pull in everything in the city till it's all mine!"

Owlette knows that if she had trained, fed, and paid attention to Birdy, this wouldn't have happened.

She turns to Birdy. "Birdy, I promise I won't let you down again. I'll build you a nest and feed and train you every day. We'll be best friends."

"The gates won't hold for long," says Owlette. "If everything flies at HQ at once, it could knock it right over."

"Owlette, we'll hold the gates while you go inside HQ and turn off the beam," says Catboy.

But that isn't going to be so easy. The doors to HQ are magnetized shut.

Luckily, Birdy has a plan. Birdy finds Luna Girl and leads her right back to HQ and into one of the Luna Beams. Luna Girl's Luna Magnet cancels out the beam, and Birdy is able to get into HQ and grab the Luna Crystals. The Luna Beams turn off!

"I'll get you next time, PJ Pests," says Luna Girl.

"Birdy and I will be waiting for you," says Owlette.

PJ Masks all shout hooray!
'Cause in the night,
we saved the day!

The next day Connor, Greg, and Amaya go to the park. Greg brings Lionel, and Owlette brings Birdy.

"Let's see what you can do," Owlette says to Birdy.

Birdy does a loop-de-loop and lands . . . right on Greg's head.

"And sit, and stay," says Amaya as everyone laughs.

Catboy Does It Again

Connor, Amaya, and Greg are leaving the museum one afternoon when they notice something strange—the people on the street are moving backward!

"It's like they're on rewind," observes Amaya.

Connor begins walking over to the people when some birds pause in midair.

"We'd better check this out," says Amaya.

"PJ Masks, we're on our way! Into the night to save the day!" the three friends say at the same time.

Amaya becomes Owlette!

Connor becomes Catboy!

Greg becomes Gekko!

At HQ, Gekko runs up to the PJ Picture Player. It shows
Romeo and his robot at the museum!
"He's returned to the scene of the crime," says Catboy.
"To the Cat-Car!" He doesn't want to waste another second.

At the museum, the PJ Masks hide and watch Romeo. He is holding a remote. Some birds are paused in front of him.

"Ugh, silly machine is still pausing things. I need to fix this glitch," he complains. Romeo shakes the remote and presses the rewind button. The birds start moving backward!

"Romeo is zapping things into rewind," says Owlette. "But why?"

"Let's find out," says Catboy as he leaps into Romeo's view.

"Catboy!" shouts Romeo. "Robot, keep those PJ pests away while I work out the glitches on my remote."

The PJ Masks jump into action. Romeo's robot is no match for them. But before they can get Romeo's remote . . .

Romeo presses the button. The PJ Masks move backward and pause in the air!

"Did Romeo just rewind us?" asks Gekko.

"I most certainly did!" Romeo gloats. "Behold, my greatest invention ever: the Rewind-O-Ray!"

"If your invention is the Rewind-O-Ray, then why are we paused?" asks Owlette.

"It's just a tiny glitch," explains Romeo. "Once it's fixed, I'll rewind you so far back that you'll be babies and you won't ever get to become PJ Masks!"

Romeo shakes his remote again and presses the rewind button. The PJ Masks travel all the way back to HQ!

"That no-good Romeo," says Catboy. "Come on! Let's go back and take him down."

But Owlette and Gekko don't think that is a good idea. "We need a plan," says Gekko. "We've got to work together."

"There's no time," says Catboy. "Now let's go!"

Back at the museum, Catboy lunges for Romeo's remote. He has to get it or Romeo will keep rewinding everything. But Romeo is too fast. He presses his remote and rewinds the PJ Masks back to HQ again!

"I almost had him that time," Catboy says.

Owlette shakes her head. "Not even close."

"You keep making the same mistake over and over. You need to slow down and think clearly," Gekko tells Catboy. "Every time you leap into action, Romeo rewinds us."

"And if he rewinds us to before we became the PJ Masks, we're doomed," adds Owlette.

"You're right," says Catboy. "It's time for a new plan. We do have a new plan, don't we?"

Owlette leans in close. "Well, we were thinking. . . ."

Soon, the PJ Masks are back at the museum. Catboy jumps out of the Cat-Car.

"Master! Master!" calls Romeo's robot. "It's the PJ Masks!"

Romeo looks up from his remote. "It's only Catboy. Get him."

"You'll have to catch me first," says Catboy. "Super Cat Speed!"

Catboy jumps on Romeo's robot and starts spinning it around. Romeo's robot spirals out of control!

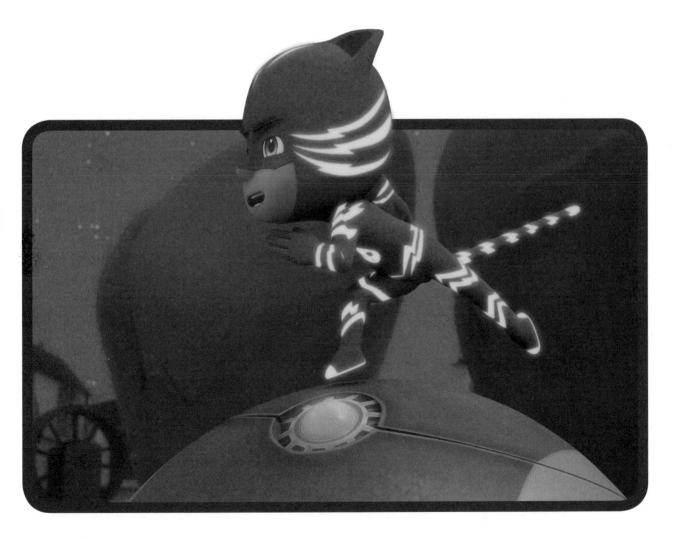

Catboy turns to Romeo, but Romeo isn't worried. He still has his remote. He zaps Catboy and freezes him in place.

"Silly kitty," Romeo taunts Catboy. "How many times do you have to make the same mistake before you realize my Rewind-O-Ray is unstoppable?"

"I'm no match for that remote," Catboy agrees. "You're just too smart for me, Romeo."

Romeo smiles. "It's hard being an evil genius, you know."

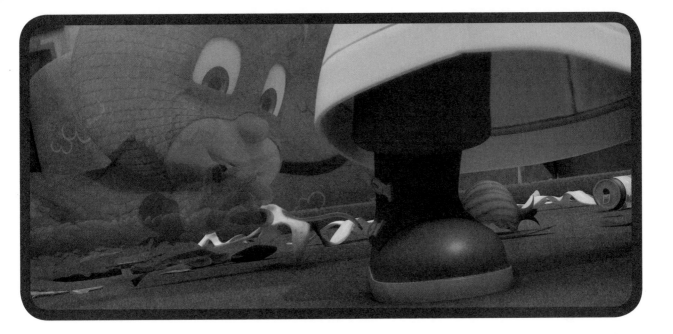

While Catboy keeps Romeo distracted, Gekko camouflages himself and places banana peels by Romeo's feet. Then Owlette flies onto the scene.

"Super Owl Wings!" she cries.

Romeo looks up . . .

. . . and all of a sudden Gekko appears!

"Boo!" says Gekko.

Romeo jumps and lands on a banana peel. He slips and slides all over the town square. As Romeo slides, he lets go of his remote. Catboy grabs it and tosses it to Gekko. Gekko presses the rewind button, and Romeo begins to slide backward!

Romeo finally lands in the garbage. "You win this time, PJ Masks!" he says.

"I want to hear that again," says Gekko, and he presses the rewind button on the remote.

"You win this time, PJ Masks!" Romeo repeats. "Hey, stop that!"

Romeo runs back to his lab. "You haven't seen the last of me, PJ Masks!"

"Maybe not," says Catboy, "but we'll be ready."

PJ Masks all shout hooray! 'Cause in the night, we saved the day!

Good Night, Heroes

Today Connor, Amaya, and Greg were going on a field trip to the museum!

"I can't wait to see the Egyptian chariot," said Greg. "The teacher says it's 3,500 years old."

"And it's made of real gold," added Connor.

But when they got to the museum, their teacher had bad news. The golden chariot had vanished! It had to be the work of a nighttime villain!

"We'll find it," said Amaya. "PJ Masks, we're on our way! Into the night to save the day!"

Amaya becomes Owlette!
Greg becomes Gekko!
Connor becomes Catboy!

The PJ Masks jumped into the Owl Glider and took off, scanning the city streets. It didn't take them long to find the chariot . . . and Night Ninja. His Ninjalinos were pulling the chariot with him in it!

"Give that chariot back," said Catboy. "Or we'll have to take it."

"You don't scare me, PJ Pests. Take me for a ride, Ninjalinos, and make it fast," Night Ninja ordered.

But the Ninjalinos were tired of being bossed around. They stopped pulling the chariot.

"What's the meaning of this?" Night Ninja asked.

"Maybe they don't like how you lead them," suggested Gekko.

"I'd be a much better leader than that," said Owlette. "We'd play and have lots of fun."

The Ninjalinos ran over to Owlette. "I'll call them my Owletteenies!" she said.

"Okay, Owletteenies—to the museum!" cried Owlette.
The Owletteenies picked up the chariot and pulled
Owlette all the way back to the museum.
"Being a leader is fun," said Owlette.

"Night Ninja will be back any moment," said Catboy when they returned to the museum. "We should hide the chariot somewhere safe."

But Owlette was having too much fun ordering around her Owletteenies.

"Owletteenies, salute your leader," she said.

Owlette wasn't happy with the way they did it.

"Owletteenies, I'm your leader," she scolded them. "You need to salute me properly. One, two, three, go!"

And so the Owletteenies did just that—they went . . . away from Owlette.

While Owlette, Catboy, and Gekko searched the museum for the Owletteenies, Night Ninja snuck in! The Owletteenies ran up to him. They decided to be Ninjalinos again. They used their Sticky-Splats to connect the chariot to a rocket ship. Now they wouldn't have to pull it!

As they blasted off, Night Ninja called out to Owlette, "So much for being a wonderful leader!"

Owlette knew Night Ninja was right. "My Owletteenies are gone, and it's all my fault," she said. "Maybe they can still help us. It's time to be a hero."

The PJ Masks followed Night Ninja in the Owl Glider.

"I'm sorry, Ninjalinos," Owlette called to them. "I'm not your leader. I'm just someone who needs your help."

All of a sudden the chariot started to break away from the rocket. The Sticky-Splats were losing their stickiness!

"We're too heavy, Ninjalinos," said Night Ninja. "All of you jump out. Now!"

But the Ninjalinos were scared.

"We have to save them!" cried Owlette. She flew the Owl Glider below the chariot. The Ninjalinos landed safely.

As for Night Ninja, there was nothing he could do. The rocket sputtered down to the ground—taking him and the chariot along with it.

When the Owl Glider landed, the Ninjalinos gave Owlette a hug. Night Ninja knew he had been wrong. "I'm sorry," he said to the Ninjalinos. He threw out his arms, and the Ninjalinos ran over to him.

"Oh, I love you too, my Ninjalinos," said Night Ninja.

The PJ Masks laughed. "You're really just a big softy," Owlette told him.

"Now let's get this chariot back to the museum," said Catboy.

The PJ Masks were getting tired, but their busy night wasn't over yet. Luna Girl was up to no good on the other side of town! She had taken the school's puppets, and her moths were putting on a puppet show just for her.

Gekko went to get the puppets back from Luna Girl, but he got caught up in her show.

"Woo-hoo!" he cheered at an exciting scene. That's when Luna Girl noticed him.

"Uh, give those puppets back," Gekko said, trying to sound serious.

"No chance!" said Luna Girl. "Moths, show him what you can do."

While Gekko was running away from Luna Girl's moths, Owlette and Catboy were taking care of something else. The PJ Masks' classmate Cameron was sleepwalking around town.

"We need to get him back to bed," said Catboy.

"Yeah, but we can't use superspeed or fly him home. That would wake him up and give him a bad shock," Owlette pointed out.

Owlette and Catboy needed Gekko's help, but he had gotten away from the moths and was more interested in the puppets than in stopping Luna Girl.

Meanwhile, Luna Girl found Cameron. Using her Luna Magnet, she turned him into a real-life puppet!

"Look at him," Luna Girl said. "He looks like a snoring dinosaur. I'm going to call him a Snore-a-saurus!"

Owlette was upset with Gekko. "Cameron wouldn't be in trouble if you hadn't been messing around with those puppets," she told him. "Are you with us?"

Gekko was determined to be a hero. Together, the PJ Masks would get Luna Girl's Luna Magnet and put Cameron back to bed without waking him up.

"Owl Wing Wind!" cried Owlette as she flapped her wings at Luna Girl. Luna Girl's moths swirled around her head. She lost control of the Luna Magnet's beam. While she was distracted, Catboy grabbed the magnet from her and threw it to Gekko.

"No, no, no, no, no!" cried Luna Girl, but there was nothing she could do. Gekko pointed the beam at Cameron and started leading him away carefully.

"Okay, let's get you to bed," said Gekko.

The night was finally quiet. Cameron was sleeping soundly in his bed, and the nighttime villains had gone home. After such a busy night, the PJ Masks sure were tired.

Owlette yawned. Catboy yawned. Gekko yawned.

PJ Masks all shout hooray!
'Cause in the night,
we saved the day!
Good night, heroes!